W9-AHX-758

Fashion Queen

by Marci Peschke

illustrated by Tuesday Mourning

PICTURE WINDOW BOOKS
a capstone imprint

Kylie Jean is published by Picture Window Books
A Capstone Imprint
1710 Roe Crest Drive
North Mankato, Minnesota 56003
www.capstonepub.com

Copyright © 2015 by Picture Window Books

All rights reserved. No part of this publication may be reproduced in whole or in part, or stored in a
retrieval system, or transmitted in any form or by any means, electronic, mechanical, photocopying,
recording, or otherwise, without written permission of the publisher.

Library of Congress Cataloging-in-Publication Data
Peschke, M. (Marci), author.
   Fashion queen / by Marci Peschke ; illustrated by Tuesday Mourning.
       pages cm. -- (Kylie Jean)
   ISBN 978-1-4795-5883-4 (hardcover) -- ISBN 978-1-4795-5881-0 (paper over board) --
   ISBN 978-1-4795-6200-8 (ebook)
   1. Fashion design--Juvenile fiction. 2. Fashion shows--Juvenile fiction. 3. Models (Persons)--Juvenile
fiction. 4. Money-making projects for girls--Juvenile fiction. 5. Families--Texas--Juvenile fiction. 6.
Texas--Juvenile fiction. [1. Fashion--Fiction. 2. Fund raising--Fiction. 3. Family life--Texas--Fiction. 4.
Texas--Fiction.] I. Mourning, Tuesday, illustrator. II. Title. III. Series: Peschke, M. (Marci) Kylie Jean.
   PZ7.P441245Fas 2015
   813.6--dc23
                                    2014022718

Summary: Inspired by the beautiful dresses at the Academy Awards show, Kylie Jean decides to try
her hand at fashion — and Lilly recruits her to model the dress she is making for a school fundraising
auction.

Graphic Designer: Kristi Carlson
Editor: Alison Deering
Production Specialist: Laura Manthe

Design Element Credit:
Shutterstock/blue67design

Printed in China.
092014   008472RRDS15

For Jenny and her sweet Celia Joy
—MP

Table of Contents

All About Me, Kylie Jean!

My name is Kylie Jean Carter. I live in a big, sunny, yellow house on Peachtree Lane in Jacksonville, Texas, with Momma, Daddy, and my two brothers, T.J. and Ugly Brother.

T.J. is my older brother, and Ugly Brother is . . . well . . . he's really a dog. Don't you go telling him he is a dog. Okay? I mean it. He thinks he is a real, true person.

He is a black-and-white bulldog. His front looks like his back, all smashed in. His face is all droopy like he's sad, but he's not.

His two front teeth stick out, and his tongue hangs down. (Now you know why his name is Ugly Brother.)

Everyone I love to the moon and back lives in Jacksonville. Nanny, Pa, Granny, Pappy, my aunts, my uncles, and my cousins all live here. I'm extra lucky, because I can see all of them any time I want to!

My momma says I'm pretty. She says I have eyes as blue as the summer sky and a smile as sweet as an angel. (Momma says pretty is as pretty does. That means being nice to the old folks, taking care of little animals, and respecting my momma and daddy.)

But I'm pretty on the outside and on the inside. My hair is long, brown, and curly.

I wear it in a ponytail sometimes, but my absolute most favorite is when Momma pulls it back in a princess style on special days.

I just gave you a little hint about my big dream. Ever since I was a bitty baby I have wanted to be an honest-to-goodness beauty queen. I even know the wave. It's side to side, nice and slow, with a dazzling smile. I practice all the time, because everybody knows beauty queens need to have a perfect wave.

I'm Kylie Jean, and I'm going to be a beauty queen. Just you wait and see!

Chapter One
Lights, Camera, Action

This is a really big weekend, because it's time for the Academy Awards! They'll be on TV this Sunday night. Seeing the movie stars all dressed up is my favorite part. Momma and I wait all year to see the glamorous gowns.

But first we have to wait all day Saturday and all through church Sunday (plus dinner afterward). Finally it's time to watch! Yay! Momma and I decide to make some snacks and treats to eat while we watch. Here is our menu:

1. Stuffed mini-potatoes

2. Buffalo chicken on a stick

3. Spinach dip with pita chips

4. Sweet-and-salty popcorn

5. Caramel brownies

Momma and I make the brownies first so we can pop them into the oven to bake while we work on the rest of our snacks. Then I get to work stirring up the spinach dip and popping the popcorn. Momma makes the sweet glaze we'll add to it. It's much too hot for me to touch, so she pours it over the fluffy kernels on cookie sheets.

The whole time we're cooking, Ugly Brother waits to taste-test the chicken.

"It's gonna be hot and spicy!" I warn him. "Are you sure you want to try it?"

He barks, "Ruff, ruff!" That means yes.

He sits back and begs, so I give him a little nibble. As soon as it hits his tongue, he starts lickin' his mouth like crazy, then hightails it straight for his water bowl.

"I told you it was spicy!" I call after him.

Just then Daddy hollers from the living room, "Sure smells good out there!"

"Is it time to eat yet?" T.J. shouts.

"Almost," Momma replies.

Snacks are definitely T.J. and Daddy's favorite part of movie awards night. Momma and I finish up and carry the food into the living room so we can snack while we watch. As soon as I set the food down, Daddy and T.J. dig in.

On TV, the stars start to arrive in their fancy limos, and the paparazzi line up with cameras to take their pictures. Momma and I *ooh* and *ahh* over every gown.

"Just look at that redheaded actress," Momma says. "That red strapless gown is just divine!"

I see the lady Momma is talking about. She is wearing long ruby-and-diamond earrings with a matching necklace. The ruby is as big as a silver dollar!

Momma's favorite look is no surprise — red is her favorite color — but my favorite look is. I bet you think I picked a pink gown, but I didn't! I fell in love with the beautiful actress wearing a long, shimmering gold gown and a diamond tiara.

"Oh, Momma, look how her tiara sparkles in the camera lights!" I say.

When all the stars have arrived, it's time for the awards. We wait to hear them call out the names of the winners. Momma lets me stay up late even though it's a school night. I feel so grown up!

As exciting as the awards show is, after a while I start to yawn, and my eyes start to drift closed. Sitting up straight, I open them wide . . . they close again. I can't believe it, but I fall asleep before the end of the show. Daddy has to carry me up to bed.

I am so sleepy at school the next day. Monday is going to be a very long day! I sure am glad when the bell rings for lunch, and we all rush out of our classroom.

I walk to the lunchroom with my friends, Cara and Paula, and my best cousin, Lucy. Inside the bright cafeteria, the walls are white and tables are bright colors. Paula hurries over to the lunch line while Cara, Lucy, and I pick a table.

"I bet you wish they had pink tables," Lucy says.

I smile. "Yup, I sure do," I say. "Pink is my best color!"

We settle for a red table close to the outside door. The tables by the door get to line up first for recess. This is important because we like to get over to the swings as fast as we can. If we don't, the boys will get to them first, and they will never let us have a turn. Swinging is our favorite part of recess!

"Did you know red is my momma's favorite color?" I ask as we unpack our lunches.

Lucy giggles. "I sure do. She's my favorite aunt!"

"Well, I didn't," Cara says. "My mom likes green best."

I dig into my pretty pink princess lunch bag and pull out one of Momma's famous grilled cheese sandwiches, a thermos of tomato soup, and a special brownie.

Paula's eyes light up. "Hey, can I have that brownie? Please, pretty please?" she asks.

I think about it carefully. The nice thing to do would be to share, so I give each friend a tiny piece of my tasty brownie.

Cara finishes her piece and turns to thank me. She has caramel on her face when she says, "This is delicious!"

"That's because that is an extra-special brownie," I tell her.

"What makes it special?" Paula asks.

"We had these brownies for our movie awards night party!" I explain. "I got to stay up late to watch it."

"You and I have something in common, Kylie Jean! I watched that with Lilly!" Lucy says. Lilly is her older sister and my best big cousin.

"You two are both so lucky," Paula says with a sigh. "My momma never lets me stay up that late."

"You should have seen the glamorous dresses and the jewels the actresses wore," I tell Paula. "Some of them looked like queens. They even had on tiaras!"

Before we know it, the bell rings, and it's time to throw away our trash and line up for recess. As I walk to the swings, I think about the beautiful actress in the long shimmering gold gown with the diamond tiara. All those gorgeous dresses have given me an idea — maybe someday I can be a real true fashion queen!

Chapter Two

Ooh La La

That afternoon after school, I can't wait to get home! I am so excited I forget to walk. Instead I run down the hallway and out to the bus. My favorite bus driver, Mr. Jim, is parked in front of the school waiting for everyone to board so we can get on the road. I climb up the steps and sit down in my favorite seat right behind him.

"Did you watch the movie awards last night, Mr. Jim?" I ask.

"Well, I did for a while," Mr. Jim replies, "but that show was so long I had to shut it off."

"Oh, no!" I exclaim. "You probably missed the most beautiful gown in the whole world!"

Mr. Jim winks at me. "Was it pink?" he asks.

Laughing, I say, "No, this time I fell in love with a gold dress. But don't you worry, pink is still my best color."

Finally Lucy gets on the bus, and all the way to Peachtree Lane we talk about fashion. I just love the colors, the styles, the shoes, and the accessories. The high-heeled sparkly shoes are my favorite. When the bus stops in front of my house, I say goodbye to Lucy, run to the front door, and wave to Mr. Jim.

Momma has leftover sweet-and-salty popcorn with an icy glass of ginger ale waiting for me as an afternoon snack when I get home. Yum! The bubbles from the ginger ale tickle my nose when I take a sip. I *love* leftover party food and so does Ugly Brother. He begs and begs for some of my popcorn.

"If I give you some of my yummy popcorn, are you going to help me later?" I ask him.

He barks, "Ruff, ruff!"

Two barks means yes, and one means no, so I give in and toss some fluffy white popcorn in his direction. Ugly Brother catches it on his tongue, swallows, and keeps begging. I pretend that he is just like a famous doggie movie star doing tricks! Pretty soon our bowl is empty.

Finally Momma comes in and asks, "Kylie Jean, do you have any homework?"

I shake my head. "No, ma'am."

"Well, run along and play, then," Momma says. "I'll call you for supper when your daddy gets home."

"Come on," I say to Ugly Brother. "I have big plans! You can help me and be my assistant. Okay?"

Ugly Brother barks in agreement. "Ruff, ruff!"

We head upstairs to my room. I grab my sketchpad, colored pencils, and markers and sit on the floor leaning against my bed. Ugly Brother sits down right beside me. He might actually be a little too close, since he has a bad habit of drooling. Paper and doggie drool don't go together, so he can't help me with this part of my plan.

Carefully I sketch out some of the gorgeous gowns I saw on the awards show. One is red, yellow, and orange and looks like a flame. Momma called the fabric ombré. Next I draw the silver gown I saw.

Once I get all of my dresses drawn, I'm going to make some of them into gowns for my Barbie dolls. I can use paper towels, tape, and markers to make the ombré dress, but how can I make the silver one?

I hold up the drawing so Ugly Brother can see it. "What do you think?" I ask. "Do you have any ideas for my design?"

He barks once. "Ruff."

Just then an idea hits my brain like thread on a needle! I can use tin foil to make a very dramatic silver gown, especially if I fold the foil to make the giant ruffles for the skirt.

I run back downstairs with Ugly Brother right behind me. We head to the kitchen where Momma has started supper. She is leaning over a big black skillet in her pink polka-dot apron. The air in the kitchen smells delicious.

When Momma sees me, she says, "No more snacks right now, sweet pea. It's almost suppertime."

"I'm not here for snacks," I tell her. "I am here to ask you for a favor. Can I please use some of your tin foil?"

"Sure!" Momma says. "Are you working on a project?"

"Yep!" I tell her. "I'm making dresses for my Barbies, just like the gowns from last night! I need the foil to make the silver dress."

"How fun!" Momma says. "I might have some other materials you can use, too. Follow me, sugar."

We head to the laundry room, and Momma opens up one of the cabinets. Wrapping paper, ribbons, and party decorations roll out across the floor.

"These could make some really beautiful ball gowns," Momma tells me. "Would you like to use some of this paper and ribbon?"

"Yes, please!" I reply excitedly. I've already got my eye on the perfect roll of pink crepe paper streamers.

I give Momma a big squeezy hug to say thank you, and she goes back to cooking while I fill two bags full of pretty paper and ribbon. Ugly Brother drags one upstairs for me, and I carry the other. I sure am grateful to have such a helpful assistant!

My first design is a hot-pink dress; I decide to make it out of layered crepe paper. I carefully wrap my Barbie in the pink creation. Oh, no! She looks like a pink mummy. I decide to get my assistant's opinion.

"Does this make Barbie look like a mummy?"
I ask Ugly Brother.

Ugly Brother stares at my Barbie and barks
twice. "Ruff, ruff."

Hmmm. I decide to add straps to the dress. Maybe that will help. Then I use my gold glitter pen to make a design on the bottom of the dress.

When I'm done, I stand my doll in front of the jewelry box on my dresser and step back to take a good look at the gown.

"Ooh la la!" I exclaim.

Ugly Brother runs around the room barking and wagging his tail. The dress is a hit! Next we start the ombré dress. First I color the paper towel with red, yellow, and orange markers to make it look like flames. When I turn around to get my scissors, I see Ugly Brother has a paper towel flame for a tongue.

"Bad doggie! Fashion is for wearing, not eating!" I tell him.

But this gives me another idea. "Were you trying to wear this dress?" I ask.

Ugly barks, "Ruff, ruff." That's a yes.

"You're just jealous of Barbie!" I say. "Would you like me to make you a new outfit, too?"

Ugly Brother barks again twice. He is so happy that he wags his tail and runs in a circle. I better get to work if I'm going to make doggie designs, too!

By the time Momma calls us for supper, our flame dress is finished. I'm going to make the silver gown next. I wonder if fashion designers can stay up past their bedtime?

Chapter Three
Strike a Pose

After supper Momma asks me what I want to wear tomorrow for picture day at school. I can't believe I forgot! I would normally *never* forget about picture day, but I have been so excited about the Academy Awards it just slipped right out of my mind.

I explain to Ugly Brother that I will have to put off planning his new outfit. I need to pick out something to wear first.

"I'm sure sorry, Ugly Brother," I say, "but your new outfit will have to wait. I have to figure out what I'm going to wear tomorrow."

Ugly Brother hangs his head in disappointment and gives me sad puppy dog eyes.

"Don't worry," I tell him. "I promise I will make your outfit as soon as I can. And in the meantime, you can help me choose the perfect outfit for picture day!"

That cheers Ugly Brother up. He barks, "Ruff, ruff," and takes off up the stairs.

I run upstairs after him. Throwing open my closet doors, I begin to pull out dresses. I try on polka dots, stripes, and leopard prints. Ugly Brother has a good eye for fashion, so after each outfit I ask, "Do you like this ensemble?"

Ensemble means outfit. I heard the reporters on the movie awards show talking a lot about each star's ensemble.

Ugly Brother barks, "Ruff." Not a winner.

I try on more and more outfits, and over and over again, Ugly Brother barks "ruff." I think maybe he forgot that two barks means yes. By now my bed is covered with a mountain of colorful rejects.

Just then an idea hits my brain like sequin trim on satin. Finally I know just what to do — wear pink! I put on a pink leopard miniskirt, a pink top with a silver sparkly heart on the front, and black boots. Then I brush my hair up into a side ponytail. It's my favorite new hairdo. Momma taught me how to fix it, and I love it!

The last thing I do is put on a pair of sparkly star earrings with a necklace. Then I twirl in front of my mirror, striking a pose with one hand on my hip. "Well, what do you think?" I ask Ugly Brother.

He barks, "Ruff, ruff, ruff!"

Three barks must mean, "Ooh la la!"

That settles it — I have the perfect picture-day outfit! I look around my room at the mess. Now I just have to put everything away so we can go to bed. I need my beauty sleep so I can look pretty for the camera tomorrow!

* * *

The next morning, I take my time getting ready. I want to look extra glam for picture day! I have to hurry to catch the bus. Lucy and Lilly are already in their seats.

"You look just like a model!" Lilly says when she sees me.

I walk down the aisle of the bus, turn, and strike my pose.

Lilly looks impressed. "Wow, little cousin, you have style *and* can strut down the runway, too!" she says.

"Practice makes perfect," I say, "so last night I tried on both my outfit and my pose."

"That hand on the hip thing makes you look like a real model," Lilly tells me.

"That's how I'll be posing for my school picture today!" I tell them.

Suddenly Lilly's face lights up. "Kylie Jean, I just got a great idea!" she says. "My home economics class is making outfits to auction off as a fundraiser for the junior/senior prom. Will you model my outfit in the fashion show next Saturday?"

I want to say yes, but I'm a little nervous since I've never been a real model before. Everything I know about modeling comes from what I've seen on TV. "What would I have to do?" I ask.

Lilly says, "Don't worry, little cousin, it will be easy-peasy. You have natural talent! Please just say yes."

"Do it!" Lucy says. "I'm too shy or else I'd be a model, too. But you'll be great, Kylie Jean!"

I consider Lilly's invitation carefully. I am already a fashion designer, but being a model too would be awesome. I really want to be a total fashionista.

"I'll do it!" I tell Lilly. "When do we get started?"

Lilly gives me a big squeezy hug, and we promise to talk about the fashion show after school. It's only two weeks away!

When our class is called to the auditorium later that day to get our pictures taken, I am ready! I pretend that the photographer is actually the paparazzi. I put my hand on my hip and flip my ponytail, posing just like I practiced.

The camera flashes, and the photographer calls, "Next!"

I walk away with a big smile. Momma will be so surprised when the pictures come in!

Chapter Four
Walk the Dogwalk

On Wednesday I had lots of homework, but today is Thursday and all I have to do is study my spelling words for tomorrow's test. I know them already, so this is the perfect time to design some doggie duds for Ugly Brother. After all, I did promise him that I would make his outfit as soon as I could.

In my room, I get out my sketchpad and pencils. As I draw, I start thinking about the fashion show. I sure hope my cousin Lilly is designing something really special for me to wear.

After a few minutes, Ugly Brother wanders in to join me. It's good timing because I'm feeling stumped. I need some inspiration for this outfit! Those handsome movie stars are still on my mind, and they all had on tuxedos.

"Would you like a formal outfit?" I ask Ugly Brother. "How about a tuxedo?"

He doesn't even bark, not yes or no.

I try again. "You'd look mighty fine in a tux . . ."

Ugly Brother tries to look at my paper, so I hold up my drawing.

He barks, "Ruff, ruff."

Phew! That means he likes the outfit I am going to make for him. Now I just need some material. Looking at Ugly Bother's big ol'  tummy, I decide it better be stretchy. I need some help."

"Momma!" I holler.

"I'm in my room, sweet pea," Momma calls back.

"Ugly Brother, you wait here while I go talk to Momma," I say. Then I dart down the hall to my parents' room.

When I tell Momma all about my dilemma, she says, "How about using an old sweater? It stretches."

"Do you have any in black?" I ask. That's what I'll need for Ugly Brother's tuxedo.

Momma disappears into her closet and comes out with one of Daddy's old black sweaters.

"Can I cut it up?" I ask.

"That old sweater has a big hole in it," Momma says. "You'd be doing me a favor if you cut it up!"

"Thanks, Momma!" I say.

I hurry back to my room and carefully cut off the sleeves of Daddy's old black sweater to make the body of Ugly Brother's tux. Next I cut two armholes in the sides. I am using my needle and thread this time. I can't sew with a machine, but I am really good with a needle and thread. Granny taught me when I was little.

"Ugly Brother, can you bring me the thread?" I ask. "Pretty pretty please?"

Ugly Brother grabs the thread in his mouth and carries it over. It's a little slobbery.

Carefully I thread the needle through the tiny hole, cut a white hanky to make a shirt front, and hand-sew a sequined bow tie from an old barrette on the front.

When I'm finished, it's time for the fitting. I try to pull the sweater tuxedo on over Ugly Brother's big belly. It's easy to figure out that trying on this outfit is *not* going to be easy. I pull and pull and pull at the tuxedo, and Ugly Brother wiggles and wiggles.

"Hold still!" I holler.

With a final pull, it slides right on. Ugly Brother looks amazing in his new duds and runs off to get his leash. He must want to go for a walk and show off his new ensemble.

When he brings me his black leather leash, I snap it on his collar. It looks so good with his new outfit! "You sure do have an eye for fashion!" I tell him.

Ugly Brother and I decide to stroll all around the neighborhood, and the neighbors all stop us to check out Ugly Brother's doggie duds. We stop, wave, and walk on. When we are almost home, I see Miss Clarabelle, my neighbor, sitting on her wide front porch.

"Have you dressed up that poor dog again?" Miss Clarabelle hollers.

"Yes, ma'am," I reply. "But this time I made the outfit all by myself!"

Ugly Brother turns in a circle and poses so she can get the full effect.

"I declare, you do have a flair for fashion, Kylie Jean," Miss Clarabelle says. "He looks very stylish! In fact, I think he is the handsomest dog I've ever seen!"

Just then an idea hits my brain like a model on a runway. I should practice my walk for the fashion show! Did you know that in Paris the models walk down a stage called a catwalk? I can use the driveway for my catwalk.

"Gotta go, Miss Clarabelle!" I call, waving goodbye. "See you later!"

Ugly Brother and I run across Miss Clarabelle's yard, carefully avoiding the pretty flowers. I start at the top of the driveway and strut all the way down to the bottom. I pause at the end to do a turn and put my hand on my hip. That's my signature move!

Ugly Brother barks enthusiastically, "Ruff, ruff!"

He thinks I'm doing great, but I'm not sure. I want a second opinion. Soon T.J. comes along.

"T.J., pretty please, can you film me with your camera phone so I can see how I'm doing?" I beg.

"Okay, lil' bit," T.J. agrees, "but you have to hurry because I'm on my way to practice."

I hurry back to the top of the driveway to start again. But every time I start my runway walk, Ugly Brother follows me down the driveway. He looks great in his tux, but it is hard to be a model with a dog distraction.

Finally I have to stop and tell Ugly Brother, "Silly dog, this is the catwalk, not the dogwalk!"

Chapter Five
Fashion Fitting

The next day is Friday, and when I get on the bus, Lilly waves me over right away. "Hey, Kylie Jean," she says. "Do you want to come over after school today? I need you to try on the dress I'm making for the fashion show."

"I'd love to!" I say. "I can't wait to see my dress and show you my runway walk. I've been practicing!"

I am so excited to see my dress, but it is such a busy day, I hardly have time to think about it again until my teacher, Ms. Corazón, tells us it's time to get ready to go home.

"Kylie Jean, the office sent a note for you to give to your bus driver," Ms. Corazón tells me. "You are going home with your cousin today!"

"Yes, ma'am, I know," I reply as I collect my note. "Thank you very much."

Mr. Jim takes the note when I hop up the steps onto his bus. "Okie-dokie, little lady," he says once he's read it over.

I spot Lilly sitting all the way in the back of the bus with the high school kids. She gives me a little wave and a wink.

I take my favorite seat in the front row right ·
behind Mr. Jim. Lucy sits with me and we talk all
the way to her house. I am so excited, I can hardly
wait to see Lilly's design, and talking helps the
time go by faster.

When we get to my cousins' house, their
momma, my Aunt Susie, has a snack waiting for
us. It looks delicious, but we decide to work first
and snack later. Lilly goes to her room to get her
design, and when she comes back, she's carrying
a dress so pink and adorable, it looks like a
Valentine.

"Yay!" I holler. "Oh, Lilly, I just love it!"

"Did you notice the top part is shaped like a
heart?" Lilly asks. "And so are the pockets on the
front of the skirt."

"That's one of my absolute favorite things about it!" I tell her.

"Stand on the coffee table, Kylie Jean," Aunt Susie says. "That way Lilly can make sure it fits."

Lilly pulls the pretty little dress over my head, and I step carefully up onto the coffee table.

Lucy holds the pincushion while Lilly pins the hem of the dress. Then she pins white lace around the hearts on the front of the dress.

When everything is all pinned up, I get to look in the mirror. I look like I am dressed for a fancy party!

"Lilly, you are a fashion genius!" I tell her.

"It's not quite finished yet," Lilly tells me. She brings out her sketchpad to show me what else she has planned, and I see that the design has little pearls sewn on the pockets. When she starts to close her sketchpad, I notice another dress. I gasp! It's a fabulous grown-up gown.

"Who is wearing that dress for the fashion show?" I ask.

"No one!" Aunt Susie says. "Lilly has been making her own prom dress, too."

"Lilly, please try on your dress!" I tell her. "Pretty please!"

Lilly laughs. "Not yet," she says. "I'm waiting to make sure every little stitch is perfect!"

"Oh, please, Lilly," I beg. "Granny always says there's no time like the present and I tried on my dress for you."

"Oh, okay!" Lilly agrees. "Wait here, and I'll model it for you since you are modeling for me!"

Lilly disappears for a few minutes, and when she comes back out, she looks like a moonbeam in her lovely silver gown. It is long and straight with a little flounce at the bottom. It has little cap sleeves with a simple elegant bodice.

Lilly twirls and admires herself in the huge mirror in the front hall. "Do you like it?" she asks.

"You look just like one of those movie stars on the red carpet!" I tell her. "But you need a little sparkle. Then you could be a real true movie star!"

Lilly smiles. "That's awful sweet of you, Kylie Jean," she says. "I would hug you if I wouldn't mess up my dress."

"I like it, too!" Lucy chimes in.

Lilly smiles at her. "Thanks, little sis," she says.

Suddenly Aunt Susie snaps her fingers. "I think I have something Lilly can borrow," she says. "Wait here."

We all wait while Aunt Susie runs up to her room. A few minutes later, she comes back in with a black velvet box. We all crowd around to see what's inside. When she opens it, I see a short diamond necklace and earrings to match.

Lilly gasps. She is so overcome by the sight of the gorgeous jewels that she can't even find her words.

But I can. "That's what I call sparkle!" I say.

Lilly puts on the earrings and necklace with a happy sigh. "Oh, they are perfect!" she says. "And now I look just like a movie star!"

Aunt Susie grabs her new camera to take some pictures of us in our fabulous dresses, and Lilly and I strike a pose. Lucy decides to get in on the action too. The camera flashes and flashes! I feel like a real movie star!

When Momma arrives to pick me up that afternoon, I can't wait to tell her all about my dress. But she has some big news!

"Miss Clarabelle wants to talk to you, Kylie Jean," Momma says. "She was so impressed by your designer doggie outfit that she wants to order one for her pup, Tess."

"Oh, boy!" I exclaim. "Let's hurry home. I have some designing to do!"

When we get home, I get right to work. I make several sketches of doggie duds before Momma finally tells me that it's time for bed. When I crawl under the covers, I fall right asleep. Being a fashion queen sure is hard work!

Chapter Six

Puparazzi

The next morning I am up before the sun peeks out. But when I knock on Momma and Daddy's door, she tells me, "Kylie Jean, it is too early to be awake on a Saturday morning!"

Ugly Brother is ready for breakfast, so we head down to the kitchen. He likes eggs with bacon, but Momma doesn't let me cook on the stove alone.

"How about cereal and toast?" I suggest.

"Ruff," Ugly Brother barks. That's a no.

"Okay, no cereal for you, just toast," I agree.

Ugly Bother likes his toast with peanut butter on it. I have Cocoa Puffs since I am a *big* chocolate lover. Then we watch cartoons until Momma gets up. When she comes down wearing her robe to make coffee, I ask, "Can we go visit Miss Clarabelle now?"

"Okay," Momma says, "but it's still pretty early, so just knock once."

"Yes, ma'am!" I say. Then I turn to my assistant. "Ugly Brother, we have an important meeting with a very special customer. Are you ready to get to work?"

He barks, "Ruff, ruff."

Ugly Brother and I slip out the back door and head across the yard to Miss Clarabelle's house. *Tip-tap*, I knock lightly on the front door. Miss Clarabelle answers right away! She and her sweet little pup Tess must have been waiting for us to arrive.

"I hope you have a wonderful design for my darling little doggie," Miss Clarabelle says when she sees me.

Before I can reply, Ugly Brother does. "Ruff, ruff."

Miss Clarabelle laughs at him. I cover my mouth with my hand to hide a little giggle. Silly Ugly Brother!

I flip through all the pages of my sketchpad and show Miss Clarabelle and Tess my designs. When I get to the sweetest little purple pup tutu with tiny diamonds sewn all over the skirt, Miss Clarabelle claps her hands.

"That's the one!" she exclaims. "I *love* it!"

Purple is Miss Clarabelle's best color, so I'm not surprised that she picked this outfit as her favorite. It even has a matching bow for Tess to wear on her collar!

Once we've decided on a design, I hurry home. I need Momma to take me to the fabric store. Now that I am making doggie designs, I will need more supplies!

When Ugly Brother and I get back to our house, Momma is waiting in the kitchen. "How did it go?" she asks.

"Fantastic!" I tell her. "I have my very first order, but I need your help."

"What do you need, buttercup?" Momma asks.

"I need to go to the Crafty Corner craft shop and get supplies," I tell her. "Would you mind driving me?"

"Of course I will, sugar," Momma says. She grabs her purse, and we're off. On our way, I make a list of things I need:

1. Purple net material
2. Elastic
3. Purple thread
4. Sparkly diamonds
5. Fabric glue

When we get to the craft store, I show Momma my list.

"You can cross off thread," Momma tells me. "I have some at home already."

We quickly gather everything else on the list, and I push the shopping buggy to the checkout counter where Momma pays for our purchases.

Back at home, I get busy making Tess's outfit. I cut and sew, cut and sew. Once the little skirt is finished, I glue the sparkly diamonds on it. Then I make an adorable fluffy bow to match for her collar.

Ugly Brother watches me while I work. He can't help much with this part, so he is keeping me company instead. While I work, I tell him all about the fashion show. It is only a week away now, and I am so excited!

"Do you think I'll be a good model?" I ask Ugly Brother.

"Ruff, ruff," he barks. I sure hope he's right!

Finally my doggie design is finished! I take it over to Miss Clarabelle's house, and we try it on Tess. She dances around showing off. Miss Clarabelle is so happy that she gives me a big squeezy hug.

"Let's take a walk to the dog park," she suggests. "I want to show this outfit off!"

Tess gets lots of attention there. Her outfit is a hit! People are so impressed that I get two more orders from new customers.

That afternoon Momma takes me back to the Crafty Corner again so I can get the supplies I need to fill my fashion orders. If this keeps up, maybe I can go into business! I could call it Kylie Jean's Doggie Designs!

On Sunday after church, I make the cutest butterfly outfit for a little pug and an adorable little red poodle skirt for a poodle. I cut and sew, cut and sew. By the time I'm finally finished, it's time for supper. I take my doggie duds downstairs to show Momma and Daddy.

"Kylie Jean, you are so creative," Momma says. "Those dog outfits are the cutest I've ever seen."

Daddy agrees. "Are there many dogs dressed up at the park?" he asks.

"There are going to be a lot more now!" I tell him.

"You better be careful, Kylie Jean," T.J. says with a laugh. "If your doggie designs get too famous you'll have puparazzi to deal with!"

Chapter Seven
Cut and Curl

When I get on the bus Monday after school, my cousin Lilly is already sitting in the back. She looks pretty as a picture in her blue jean skirt and black cowboy boots. Most high school kids are stuck-up. Some of them are even mean to the little kids! Not Lilly, though; she's as sweet as sugar. Momma always says pretty is as pretty does, and Lilly is pretty on the inside *and* the outside.

Lilly waves to me like she's got something important to say, so I hurry to the back of the bus, too.

"Hey, there, little cousin," Lilly says. "I made us appointments to get our hair done tomorrow. I want you to have a special hairstyle for the fashion show, and I'm going to get my hair cut."

"Oh, boy!" I tell her.

"Do you think your momma could pick us up and drop us off at the Cut and Curl after school?" Lilly asks.

"I'm sure she won't mind," I say. "She's used to being my driver, but I better ask if it's okay. I'll call you after I get home."

"Sounds like a plan," Lilly says.

Giving a quick little beauty queen wave, I smile and head back to the front of the bus.

"Hurry up, little gal!" Mr. Jim calls. "It's time to roll. You better get in your seat!"

When I hop off the bus on Peachtree Lane, Momma has my afternoon snack all ready. While I eat my tangerine, I ask her if she can drive us to the Cut and Curl.

"Of course I can," Momma agrees. "I have some errands to run anyway."

I decide to text Lilly to let her know Momma will be happy to drive us to our appointment. Momma lets me use her cell phone.

U R going 2 B happy, I type. *Momma will drive us.*

Lilly texts back: *Thx. C U tomorrow!*

The next day after school, Momma drops us off at the salon. The Cut and Curl is one of my favorite places. It is so pink! It has pink paint and pink wallpaper, and fancy white chairs with pink cushions line the edge of the room.

"Y'all have a seat," Miss Norma tells us. "I'll be finished before you know it."

"Yes, ma'am!" Lilly and I say.

We sit on the soft pink velvet seats to wait for our turn. Lilly looks at a magazine while we are waiting. I look all around the room. Hanging on one wall are pictures of girls with pretty hairdos. Suddenly I realize the pictures on the wall are photos of girls we know!

I tug on Lilly's arm and point to the pictures. "Hey, isn't that Ruby Mae Butler?" I say. "We know her."

"I wonder why they all have short hair?" Lilly asks.

"Miss Norma, can you explain how a picture of Ruby Mae got on your wall?" I ask.

Miss Norma smiles. "Well, all those girls are so sweet, they cut off their hair to donate it to Locks of Love," she explains.

"Locks of Love?" I say. "What's that?"

"Locks of Love makes wigs for cancer patients," Miss Norma explains. "All those girls cut off their hair so it could be used for wigs."

"That is so sad!" I say. "I wish I could cut off my hair and help, too!

"Whoa, little cousin," Lilly says. "I don't think we can cut off all your hair without your momma's permission."

I sigh. "But I really wanted to help."

Lilly hesitates, then says, "What if I cut my hair, and we donate it together?"

I sure am surprised! "Oh, thank you, Lilly!" I exclaim. "You are the best big cousin ever! I just love your plan!"

Lilly picks her new hairstyle from the magazine she has been looking at. Then Miss Norma washes her hair, pulls it back in a long ponytail, and *snip-snip*, she cuts it all off. After that, she cuts the back of Lilly's hair super short and leaves the front a little longer. Her new short haircut is called a bob. It is so cute!

It's my turn next. First I get a shampoo. The water is warm and soapsuds tickle my ears. Then I take a seat in the chair, and Miss Norma swings a pink cape over me.

Miss Norma has to raise the salon chair up a bit higher so she can fix my hair. The chair makes a *pump, pump, pump* sound as it goes up, up, up.

Miss Norma uses the blow dryer and a round brush to curl my hair. She twirls the brush around my hair, but it doesn't hurt.

Next there is a flurry of hairspray, and then Miss Norma uses the curling iron to twist long, pretty curls all down my back. Finally she ties a pretty pink ribbon around my head like a bow.

"You sure look like a little model to me!" Lilly says. "That pink bow will be perfect with your dress. We just have to fix your hair the same way the day of the fashion show!"

Before we leave, Miss Norma uses her camera to take a photo of Lilly's new bob for her picture wall. I get to be in the picture, too!

"Say cheese!" Miss Norma says.

Lilly and I both smile, but instead of "Cheese!" we say, "Fashion!"

We all laugh. Just then, I spot Momma's car out front. The little bell on the door rings as we leave the salon.

When we get in the car, Momma is so surprised by Lilly's big haircut. "You look as pretty as a picture, Lilly!" she says.

Lilly blushes. "Thank you," she says. Then she asks, "Can I borrow Kylie Jean again on Thursday night? We're having a fashion show rehearsal at the convention center to practice."

"Sure thing," Momma says.

I can't wait! Look out runway, here I come!

Chapter Eight
Practice and Pointers

It's finally Thursday! I have been anxiously waiting for rehearsal day to arrive. I thought it would never get here.

In the afternoon, Momma and I head over to the Jacksonville Convention Center to practice for the fashion show. Lilly is going to meet us there, so we wait for her in the lobby. Several girls from Lilly's sewing class are already there with their models. They all look a little nervous, just like me!

Just then, Lilly walks in. "Hey, little cousin," she says.

Before I can say hey back, Lilly's friends all crowd around her like bees on a sweet-smelling blossom. Lilly's new short hairstyle causes quite a stir.

"Oh, I just love it!" one girl says.

Another says, "It's so adorable. Now we're all going to want to cut our hair!"

Lilly is starting to blush. I think all of this attention is beginning to make her feel a little embarrassed.

Just then, a tall older lady claps her hands to get everyone's attention. She introduces herself as Mrs. Brooks, the fashion show director.

"Mrs. Brooks used be a model a long time ago," Lilly whispers. "Now she gives etiquette classes — that means how to mind your manners."

The director walks over to us, and Lilly introduces me. "Mrs. Brooks, this is my model and cousin, Kylie Jean Carter."

Mrs. Brooks shakes my hand, saying, "It is nice to make your acquaintance, young lady."

Mrs. Brooks has a kind smile and she is wearing pink lipstick! I like her already. I want to make a good impression, so I try to remember everything Momma told me to do when you meet someone new.

"Very nice to meet you, too, ma'am," I say.

Momma smiles, and I know she's proud of me.

Mrs. Brooks calls the models over for some directions. "I want everyone to line up by height, from shortest to tallest," she says. "Then you'll all walk on the stage so I can see how you do and give you some pointers before Saturday's show."

As we line up, I see the models are all ages. Some are tall, and some are small. I am kind of short, so I will be second in line.

The first girl walks to the end of the catwalk and back. She is so scared that she never ever looks up.

"That was good," Mrs. Brooks tells her, "but when you are walking, look for your family in the audience instead of looking down. You will see a friendly face and not feel so nervous. That's a good tip for everyone."

Then it's my turn! I am already so nervous that my hands are getting sweaty. I close my eyes and imagine that I am walking down the runway in Paris, France. Standing tall, I stride across the stage flashing my best beauty queen smile. At the end of the runway, I do a twirl and put my hand on my hip.

Mrs. Brooks looks impressed. "Have you been practicing?" she asks me. "That was an excellent walk!"

"Thank you, ma'am!" I say. "I have been. My momma always tells me that practice makes perfect."

Mrs. Brooks smiles. "Your momma is right," she agrees. "Girls, remember that — your momma is *always* right. Kylie Jean, can you walk again so the other girls can see?"

"I'd love to!" I say.

I do my runway walk again, and when I get to the end, I strike a pose. Momma is waiting with her camera to take my picture. She is trying to be just like the paparazzi!

The other models take their turns too. Some of them sprint across the stage like they are in a race.

"Remember to walk slowly," Mrs. Brooks tells us. "The fashion show is a fundraiser for the prom, and people need time to see the outfits so they can decide if they would like to buy them."

When the rehearsal is finished, Mrs. Brooks tells us that we'll need to be at the convention center two hours before the fashion show starts on Saturday. That will give us time to get our hair and makeup done.

I can't contain my excitement. "We get to wear makeup!" I blurt out.

Momma shushes me until Mrs. Brooks finishes talking, but I don't hear anything else. I am busy daydreaming about pink eye shadow.

When we get home, it is already past my bedtime since it's a school night. I put on my PJs and climb into bed quick as can be. I need to get my beauty sleep, because there is only one more day until the fashion show!

Chapter Nine
Fashion Show Fabulosity

On Saturday morning I wake up early.
Excitement is buzzing through me like lightning
in a summer storm. The fashion show is this
afternoon! I wish the hands on the clock had
wings so the time could just fly by!

Momma makes breakfast for me, and I watch
cartoons for a bit. After that I take Ugly Brother for
a walk. The clock doesn't seem to be moving at all.

Up in my room, Momma helps me pick out some shoes to wear. We both agree that my pink sandals will look perfect with the dress Lilly made. Then I spend some time with my Barbie trying on some new fashion designs I made.

Finally Momma calls, "Kylie Jean, it's time to go."

"I'm coming!" I shout.

Before I go, I give Ugly Brother a big squeezy hug. He has been a wonderful assistant, but dogs can't attend fashion shows.

On the short drive over to the convention center, Momma reminds me about the tips Mrs. Brooks gave us. "Remember to look up and walk slowly," she says.

"Don't worry, Momma," I tell her. "I am ready to rock the catwalk!"

Momma laughs. "I believe you!" she says. "Practice makes perfect, and you have been practicing nonstop."

When we arrive, there are already lots of cars in the parking lot.

"Are we late?" I cry.

Momma shakes her head. "No, those are the cars of the other models and designers," she says.

Phew! I am so relieved. Inside the convention center, people are zipping around setting things up for the show. Momma leads me to the dressing rooms behind the stage. Lilly is waiting for me there.

"Just in time, little cousin!" she says. "I sure hope someone wants to buy my dress today!"

"I am going to look so pretty in your dress, I just know you're going to sell it!" I tell her.

Lilly has the dress in a clear plastic bag so that it won't get dirty. The little pearl buttons on the pockets look so cute.

"I want to put it on right now!" I say, reaching for the bag.

But Lilly stops me. "Wait just a minute," she says. "Hair first, then dress, and makeup last."

I sigh and say, "Okay."

We find an empty dressing room table. Lilly has a huge bag filled with hairspray, brushes, and a curling iron. She fixes my hair just like Miss Norma did with long curls in the back and a pink ribbon tied into a bow.

"You look pretty as a picture!" Momma tells me.

"Just wait until she gets dressed and has her makeup on," Lilly says. "Then you'll get the full effect."

Momma and Lilly help me carefully slip the pretty dress over my head. Then I buckle on my pink sandals. They look perfect with the dress! Next I sit on a tall stool while Lilly gives me a little pale pink eye shadow and some pink lip gloss. Finally she uses a fluffy brush on my cheeks to give me just a hint of pink blush.

When she's finished, I hop down off the stool so Momma can straighten the dress.

"Okay, take a twirl and let's see how you look," Momma says.

I twirl and twirl. Then I stop and pose with my hand on my hip.

"Gorgeous!" Momma and Lilly exclaim.

It's almost time for the show to start, so Momma goes out to wait in the audience with Daddy, Lucy, and Aunt Susie. The other girls are still getting ready, and the room is noisy. I am crossing my fingers that someone pays a lot for Lilly's sweet dress.

Soon it's time! Everyone has jitters as we line up. My hands are a little sweaty again. Mrs. Brooks has music playing, and there is an announcer that is going to describe the outfits as we walk on the stage. After the show, all the dresses will be hung in the lobby next to bidding cards so folks can buy them.

I watch the first girl walk out across the stage. She remembers to look up.

I'm next! I take a deep breath just as Mrs. Brooks taps me on the shoulder. It's my turn to step up on the catwalk — I mean stage. Walking out, I smile widely. Right away I find Momma, Daddy, T.J., Aunt Susie, and Lucy sitting in the audience.

With my hands tucked into the heart-shaped pockets on my dress, I walk slowly and confidently to the end of the stage. Then I do a fancy twirl and stop to place one hand on my hip. I just can't resist giving a beauty queen wave — nice and slow, side to side — with the other hand. The audience loves my pose. They cheer as I turn to walk back.

"Good job, young lady!" Mrs. Brooks says when I come off the stage. "I like your spunky charm."

One good thing about being second in line is that you get to watch the rest of the show without being nervous! The other models all do a great job too. Everyone remembered the pointers Mrs. Brooks gave us.

When the show is over, we change faster than hummingbirds fly! All of the outfits are rushed out to the lobby to be purchased. Momma helps me change, and we go out to see who is going to buy Lilly's dress.

At first I don't see it anywhere. But then I spot Lilly and the rest of our family standing near a huge line of people. I still can't see the dress, but Lilly waves us over. She is so excited!

"Just look at all these people that want to buy our dress, Kylie Jean!" Lilly says.

Daddy winks at me. "I wonder who will get it?" he says.

When the last person in line hands in her bidding card, Daddy steps up and writes something on a bidding card of his own. Then he hands it to Lilly.

Lilly squeals. "One hundred dollars!" she shouts. "Thank you, thank you!"

Mrs. Brooks comes right over. "Congratulations, Lilly," she says. "One hundred dollars is the most money anyone has bid for a dress today!"

"Yay!" I shout. "Lilly, your dress is the best!"

Lilly gives me a high five. "We make a good team, Kylie Jean," she says.

Then an idea hits me like pearl buttons on a pocket. "Daddy, what are you going to do with Lilly's dress?" I ask him.

Daddy smiles at me. "I bought it for my very own little fashion queen!" he says.

I give Daddy a big squeezy hug. I just *love* being the queen of everything, especially fashion!

Marci Bales Peschke was born in Indiana, grew up in Florida, and now lives in Texas with her husband, two children, and a feisty black-and-white cat named Phoebe. She loves reading and watching movies.

When **Tuesday Mourning** was a little girl, she knew she wanted to be an artist when she grew up. Now, she is an illustrator who lives in Utah. She especially loves illustrating books for kids and teenagers. When she isn't illustrating, Tuesday loves spending time with her husband, who is an actor, their two sons and one daughter.

Glossary

accessory (ak-SES-ur-ee)—a small item worn with clothes that adds to the overall outfit; items like jewelry, scarves, or belts

auction (AWK-shuhn)—a type of sale where the item goes to the person who offers the most money for it

bodice (BOD-iss)—the upper part of a dress, which covers the chest, separate from the skirt and sleeves

dilemma (duh-LEM-uh)—a difficult problem that is hard to solve

etiquette (ET-i-kit)—the rules of good manners and polite behavior

ombré (ohm-BRAY)—a type of dyeing where the colors gradually fade into one another

paparazzi (pah-puh-RAHT-see)—photographers who take pictures of celebrities

pincushion (PIN-koosh-uhn)—something a designer or person who sews uses to stick their pins in, holding the pins until they need them

pose (POHZ)—a special position that someone holds so that they can be photographed, painted, or drawn

rehearsal (ri-HUR-suhl)—a practice, especially before the performance, to make sure everyone knows what to do

Talk!

1. Kylie Jean and her mom made snacks for the family to eat while they watched the Academy Awards. What kind of snacks does your family like to eat? Which is your favorite?

2. Would you rather be a model or a designer or both? Talk about it!

3. Lilly donated her hair to Locks of Love so that it could be made into a wig for someone who has cancer. Have you ever donated your hair? Talk about how you felt before and after. If you haven't done it, would you like to someday?

Be Creative!

1. Kylie Jean makes her own designs for Ugly Brother, Tess, and several other dogs. Pretend you're in her shoes, and describe the doggie designs you would make. Don't forget to include your sketches!

2. Think about what your dream outfit would look like. Draw a picture of it, and then write a paragraph about what makes it special.

3. Pretend that you're planning your very own fashion show! What would the clothes look like? What kind of decorations would you have? Who would come to the show?

This is the perfect treat for any Fashion Queen!
Just make sure to ask a grown-up for help.

Love, Kylie Jean

From Momma's Kitchen

SWEET-AND-SALTY CARAMEL POPCORN

YOU NEED:

- 4 quarts of popped popcorn
- $1/2$ cup of butter
- 1 cup of packed brown sugar
- $1/4$ cup light corn syrup
- $1/2$ tsp. of salt
- $3/4$ tsp. of baking soda

- A grown-up helper
- A brown paper bag
- Waxed paper

1. Put the butter, brown sugar, corn syrup, and salt into a microwave-safe bowl. With the help of a grown-up, heat the mixture in the microwave for two to three minutes or until it's bubbling. Stir, then add the baking soda.

2. Place the popped popcorn into the paper bag and have your grown-up pour the caramel mixture on the popcorn. Fold the top of the bag over several times, then shake gently!

3. Once popcorn is thoroughly coated, have your grown-up pour the popcorn onto waxed paper, and spread it out with a spatula. Let it cool until the caramel is set, then enjoy your salty-sweet caramel popcorn!

Yum, yum!

THE FUN DOESN'T STOP HERE!

Discover more at www.capstonekids.com

- Videos & Contests
- Games & Puzzles
- Friends & Favorites
- Authors & Illustrators

Find cool websites and more books like this one at www.facthound.com. Just type in the Book ID: **9781479558834** and you're ready to go!